Dedicated to my mom, Carol, thank you for those ....
–Marjuan Canady

For my nephew, Hamzah, may your eyes never get bigger than your tummy.
–Nabeeh Bilal

Special Thanks to
Davie Yarborough, Candice Taylor, and Tatiana Johnson
This book could not have been done without you

Callaloo: A Jazz Folktale / by Marjuan Canady.

Character and Illustrations by Nabeeh Bilal.

Based on the play, *"Callaloo: A Jazz Folktale"* by Marjuan Canady.

www.callaloothebook.com

CALLALOO

A Jazz Folktale

by Marjuan Canady

Illustrated by Nabeeh Bilal

On one hot New York City summer day, Winston ate a bowl of his favorite dish, **Callaloo.**

Winston's eyes were always
bigger than his tummy. But there
was just something magical about
his auntie's Callaloo.

It was a family recipe
passed down from Winston's
grandmother to his auntie.

"**Winston!**" said his auntie, "*What you got a belly of a goat? You ate all the callaloo! Go down to the* **roti** *shop on Flatbush Avenue and pick me up some more* **dasheen bush**."

Winston walked to the subway.

"Delicioso! Compra una Icee!"

"Delicious! Buy an Icee!" shouted
the icee lady. "Ruff!" barked Cosmo,
the neighborhood dog.

While devouring two coco Icees,
Winston heard a whisper,
"Winston!" Winston!"

He looked to his left, to his right, and to his back.

"Where did that voice come from?" thought Winston.

He shrugged, then hopped on the train and headed to the roti shop.

Sitting patiently, Winston gazed out the
subway window. His little eyes grew big.

"Where did all the familiar city
buildings disappear to?" he thought.

For he was no longer in New York
but now on the quaint Caribbean
island of Tobago.

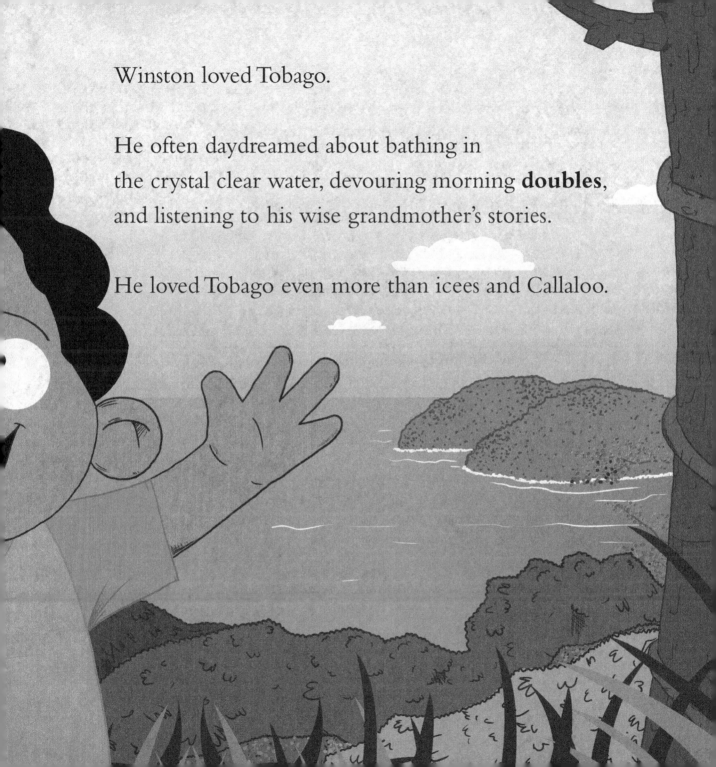

Winston loved Tobago.

He often daydreamed about bathing in
the crystal clear water, devouring morning **doubles**,
and listening to his wise grandmother's stories.

He loved Tobago even more than icees and Callaloo.

He could hear his grandmother calling him.
"Winston!" said Grandmother, *"The sun is
almost set, go down to da river over so and bring me
two crab. Me need it for me Callaloo."*

As he approached the river, Winston thought,
"Wow! Look at all these crabs!
My grandmother can cook them all for me.
I'll bring back four instead of two!"

Suddenly, a menacing shadow appeared
through the trees.

"Little Boy! Why are you stealing from my forest?!" bellowed **Papa Bois**, peace keeper and protector of all the animals in the forest.

"Aaaaah!" screamed Winston, as he ran off before Papa Bois could utter another word.

The day grew to night.
As Winston stopped to catch his breath,
he saw a man covered in black paint.
As the man inched closer to him he noticed
his curly finger nails and hairy face.

"A werewolf!" cried Winston. It was a **Lagahoo**!

"*Aooooooh*" howled the Lagahoo.
Frightened, Winston took off into the night,
running faster and faster towards a flickering light
in the distance.

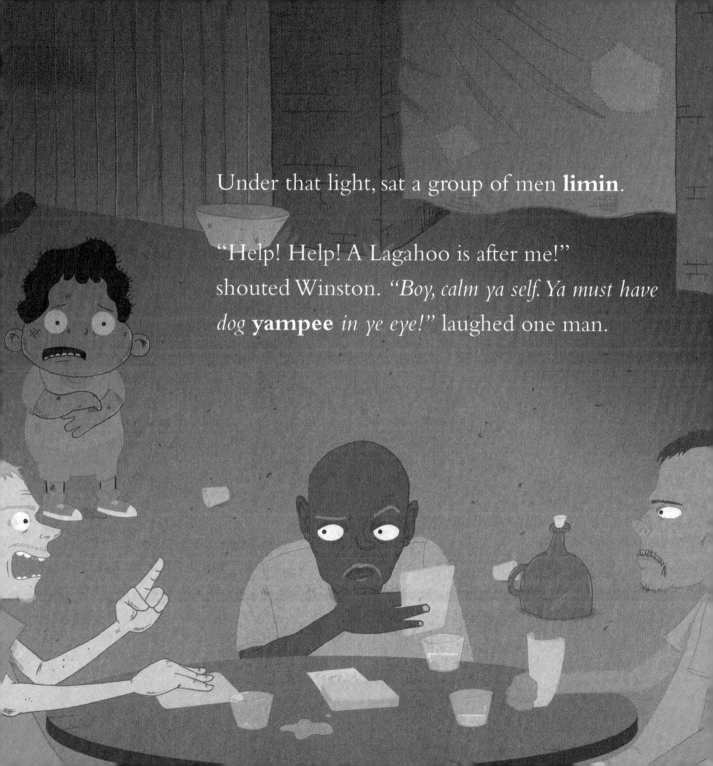

Under that light, sat a group of men **limin**.

"Help! Help! A Lagahoo is after me!" shouted Winston. *"Boy, calm ya self. Ya must have dog* **yampee** *in ye eye!"* laughed one man.

As the men laughed, Winston noticed the figure of
a beautiful woman walking alone.

"Excuse me gentlemen" interrupted Winston,
"that woman over there seems to be lost!"

"Stay Away from she!" screamed a man.

*"She a **La Diablesse**! Look at she cow hoof!"*
Winston stopped dead in his tracks.

"Don't stare at she!" yelled another man.

Winston and the men hid their faces but they could
still hear the thumping of her cow hoof inching
closer and closer and closer. Until...

POOF! She was gone!

The eldest man stared deep into Winston's eyes and said,

"You are bad luck little boy.
Get from here Nah!"

As Winston ran off, he came to a fork in the road.

He looked to his left, to his right, and to his back.

...He was lost.

His gut told him to go right.
But the more he walked,
the more he grew tired.

"What is that?" said Winston.

Covering his eyes and ears,
he heard a screeching hiss
followed by a blinding
flash in the night sky!

It was a **Soucouyant**: an old lady by day,
but vampire by night!

Pain struck his little arms.

His body grew weak and his tummy turned sick.

His arm had turned black and blue.

The Soucouyant had
chooked him!

Winston was so sick,
he fell into a deep sleep.

By morning, he woke
on the grainy beach sand to find
his arm had magically healed.

Gazing at his reflection in the ocean, he saw a
woman staring back at him.

It was **Mama D'lo**, wife of Papa Bois
and protector of all the sea animals.

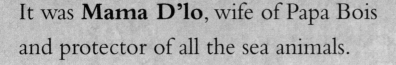

"Winston!" snickered Mama D'lo,
"*Your greed troubles me.*"

"I am sorry…" pleaded Winston.

"You were sent to me to learn a lesson!
Now if you return my crabs, I'll remove the spell that was
placed on you. If not, you will suffer the consequences!"

Winston obeyed and returned her crabs. One by one, the
crabs swam to Mama D'lo splashing around their Queen.

Just like that, the spell was broken.

Mama D'lo magically returned Winston back to his grandmother.

Winston's grandmother was **vex** that he had returned with no crabs. *"Winston, what is this? What will we eat with our Callaloo?"* said Grandmother.

"Very well, go out to me garden over so and get me one bushel of dasheen boy. No more, no less."

As Winston walked to his grandmother's garden to pick the dasheen bush, he heard a familiar whisper.

"*Winston! Winston!*"

He saw two backwards feet and a mushroom head poking out of the bushes. It was a **Douen**. *"Winston! I'll give you more dasheen bush, if you play with me"* said the douen.

But he remembered Mama D'lo's words and Grandmother's request.

So without hesitation,
he ran as fast as he could back home!

He ran and ran and ran!

He ran so fast that he ran right into Irene's Roti Shop on Flatbush Avenue!

That night, Winston and his auntie
ate a delicious Callaloo dinner
with some authentic Caribbean
dasheen bush!

...and he never again took
more than he needed.

Something magical lay within that Callaloo.

Glossary:

Callaloo (*Cal-a-loo*): a Caribbean spinach dish originating from West Africa.

Chook (*Chook*): A common word used in Trinidad and Tobago meaning to get poked with a sharp object.

Dasheen Bush (*Da-sheen Bush*): A main ingredient in callaloo. Another name for the taro plant leaves originating from South India and Southeast Asia.

Doubles (*Duh-bles*): A common Trinidad and Tobago fast food sandwich made with flat fried bread and Indian curried chick peas called chana.

Limin (*Lime-in*): A common word used in Trinidad and Tobago meaning to hang out.

Roti (*Ro-tee*): A flat bread eaten in the Caribbean originating from India.

Yampee (*Yam-pee*): A patois word used in Trinidad and Tobago referring to the cold in one's eye.

Vex (*Vex*): A common word used in Trinidad and Tobago meaning to become extremely angry.

Douen (*dwen*): A folkloric character of Trinidad and Tobago; an unbaptized child that lures children into the forest. It has a mushroom head and backwards feet, similar to the Spanish duende or goblin.

La Diablesse (*la-ja-bless*): A folkloric character of Trinidad and Tobago who casts spells on her victims, possessing one human foot and a cow's hoof. Similar to Erzulie, the Haitian spirit of love.

Lagahoo (*la-ga-who*): A mythical shape shifting folklore character of Trinidad and Tobago. Similar to the Germanic werewolf and French loup-garou.

Mama D'lo (*mama-glo*): A French word meaning "mother of the water"; a half woman, half snake, folkloric character of Trinidad and Tobago. Similar to West African spirits Yemeya and Mami Wata.

Papa Bois (*papa-bwah*): A French patois word meaning "father wood"; a half man, half horse folklore character of Trinidad and Tobago meaning protector of the forest.

Soucouyant (*sue-koo-yah*): A folkloric character of Trinidad and Tobago; an old woman by day and vampire by night. Casting spells on her victims, she flies as a fireball. Similar to the French vampire.

www.callaloothebook.com

CPSIA information can be obtained at www.ICGtesting.com
Printed in the USA
BVOW10s1106010914

364979BV00001B/1/P

9 780615 951584